i WONDER ABOUT ALLAH

I Wonder About Allah (Book One)

Published by
THE ISLAMIC FOUNDATION

Distributed by
KUBE PUBLISHING LTD
Tel +44 (01530) 249230, Fax +44 (01530) 249656
E-mail: info@kubepublishing.com
Website: www.kubepublishing.com

First published in Turkey by Uğurböceği Publications, a Zafer Publication Group imprint, in 2008.

Author Özkan Öze
Translator Selma Aydüz
Series Editor Dr Salim Aydüz
Illustrator Sevgi İçigen
Book design Zafer Publishing & Nasir Cadir
Cover Design Fatima Jamadar

Printed by Imak Ofset, Turkey

A Cataloguing-in-Publication Data record for this book is available
from the British Library

ISBN 978-0-86037-592-0
eISBN 978-0-86037-543-2

I WONDER ABOUT ALLAH

Özkan Öze

Translated by Selma Aydüz
Illustrations: Sevgi İçigen

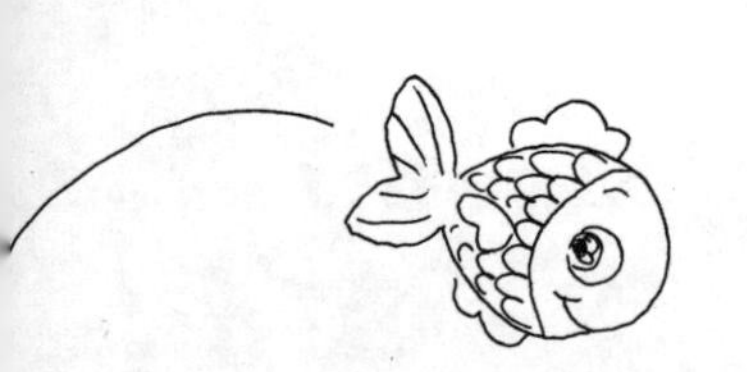

Contents

Foreword

THE STORY OF the "I Wonder" series started one day with my son asking me, "Why can't I see Allah, dad?" He asked this question at such an unexpected time that I didn't know what answer to give him.

I actually knew the answer. But when he asked so suddenly, I just said, "Umm, well..." He opened his eyes wide and started staring at me as if to say *Come on, give me the answer!* I beat around the bush for a while. You know, I was humming and hawing. In the end, I said, "Your eyes are so small, yet Allah is so big! This is the answer to the question. Because of this, you can't see Allah!"

"Oh, really?" he said. He turned his Spiderman toy around in his hands. Then, as if he hadn't said anything, he went to his room. He was only five years old…

Perhaps, for a child his age, this answer was enough. At the time, I had handled the situation. However, as he got older, he would ask heaps of new questions about Allah. In that case, I had to start preparing straight away.

So, that is how I started the "I Wonder" series.

The best thing about this book is that not only my kids, but kids from around the world can read my answers.

The "I Wonder" series' first and second books consist of answers I have given to questions about Allah.

In the third book, you will find answers to questions about our dear Prophet, peace be upon him.

The fourth book is about our holy book, The Qur'an.

As for the fifth book, the topic is death and life after death. In particular, you will find answers to questions you have about heaven.

In the sixth book, I brought together answers to questions about belief in fate.

The last book of the series is about angels.

Have I answered all the questions about all these topics? Of course not!

I only tried to answer the most frequently asked and the most important ones. But the questions I gave answers to will enlighten you in terms of the questions I didn't manage to answer as well.

My aim from the start wasn't to answer all questions; it was so that when a question comes to mind, you have the correct logic and viewpoint to approach it.

I think we largely achieved this. After reading this book, you will see that questions don't frighten you as much as before.

You will bravely ask the questions you thought were the hardest to answer, and soon you will see that you can't think of a question that doesn't have an answer.

You should never be afraid of asking questions, and don't ever give up asking questions! Because a question is a key. Every question opens a door for you. And behind every door is a whole other world.

Hang onto the question's tail and pull as much as you can. A huge answer will follow it.

Furthermore, asking a question is also a prayer.

Asking a question is saying, "I want to learn!", "I want to understand!", "I want to know better and love more!"

Make sure you do these types of prayers a lot so that your mind and heart is filled with the light of knowledge; so that your path is always bright.

The "I Wonder" Series have been written using the works of the great Muslim scholar Said Nursi (1878-1960). The answers given to the questions and the examples to help you understand the topics have all been taken from his *Risale-i Nur* books. You can easily reach these valuable works through the internet.

Özkan Öze
İstanbul, 2012

Why can't I see Allah?

DO YOU WANT to see Allah? Don't be afraid to say, "Yes, I want to see Allah," because I understand how you feel. I want to see Allah too.

I, too, wonder about Allah, who hung the glistening sun above the earth like a lamp.

Is it possible not to wonder about Allah, who lit up the dark night sky with the moon and millions of stars?

Look at the earth! A humongous basketball hanging in space. No, no, I am wrong. It is not just hanging; it's orbiting the sun at extraordinary speeds. I also want to see Allah, who keeps the earth in its orbit without allowing it to fall.

How could we not wonder about Allah, who wraps the earth with the sky?

Who wouldn't wonder about Allah, who makes heavy clouds float in the sky as if they're not carrying seas and rivers of water?

What is more reasonable than wanting to know about and wanting to see Allah, who allows rain to fall from the clouds, who creates each snowflake to be different from another?

Look at those trees! They drink muddy water through their roots, yet cherries as sweet as honey, mouth-watering apples, succulent pears and pomegranates with hundreds of seeds, grow out of their branches.

Who wouldn't want to see Allah, who creates and does all these things?

"Why can't I see Allah?" you ask. You're completely justified in wanting to see Him.

I feel the same way.

I want to see Allah too! I want to know Him better and love Him more.

Look at all these flowers: daisies, carnations, roses – all different from each other.

Of course you wonder about Allah, who created all these flowers, all more beautiful than the other, all so colourful and with their individual fragrances.

Oh no, I almost forgot!

What about the sparrows chirping in the trees?

Think about the tall storks. What about the seagulls you throw your bread at?

Close your eyes for a second and think about all the birds you have seen. Think about how they beat their wings when they fly, and how they float with the wind.

Some have pleasant voices.

Some have magnificent feathers.

And some make spectacular nests and feed their chicks.

I wonder more than anything about Allah, who created those birds and gives them beaks, wings and voices. You want to see Him too and you want to know why you can't.

You're completely right. We're both right.

Isn't it a miracle how a tiny cell multiplies into many and develops into a baby in your mum's tummy?

Your hands, fingers, your face, eyes, mouth, tongue, ears, your hair and your eyebrows, are all the result of two cells combining and then splitting and multiplying inside your mum's belly.

Yet, these are such hard and complicated things.

Your heart, lungs, kidneys, brain – all of your organs have been perfectly placed and are made to work. Now, you're curious about Allah, and you are wondering, "Why can't I see Allah, who created me and everything around me so perfectly?"

You're right, you're completely right.

Okay, now I'm going to try to answer your questions, but first I need to remind you of a few things. You need to be patient.

Because, my friend, you haven't asked a question that can be easily answered.

Your question is very big.

And, of course, such big questions have big answers.

Everything has a limit

There's a limit to everything you can do. For example, what's the maximum weight you can lift? Twenty, twenty-five, thirty kilograms... but never a hundred. This is because the muscles in your arms and in the rest of your body have a limit to how much they can take. You can never go beyond this limit. If you try to go over the limit, you will either break a bone or get squashed under the weight.

Your ears have a limit too. You can hear your teacher in your classroom, but you can't hear the teacher in the class across from you.

Your voice also has a limit. You can shout as much as you want, but if you have a grandma in a far away village, she will not hear you. If you want to talk to her, you must phone her or visit her village. Of course, your grandma could come over to you too.

What about your legs?

How fast can you run?

Are you as fast as a leopard?

Of course, your legs also have a limit.

Even if you run very fast, after some time you will get tired and you will have to stop.

How many glasses of milk can you drink at once? Two, maybe three, right?

Because your stomach has a limit too.

Now, here's a question for you:

3 x 5

Okay, okay. You don't have to laugh! I know this is a very easy question.

Well, tell me the answer to this question:

2134594 x 777

What happened?

It's pretty hard to answer this question without a calculator. But don't worry, this is completely normal, because your mind also has a limit.

Some things you understand easily.

Some questions you can answer straight away. But you can't understand everything that easily, and you can't answer every question straight away.

Some things you will never know on your own. You learn from those who do know. Because, like I said, even your mind has a limit.

As you probably guessed, it's time to have a look at your eyes.

Don't you think they have a limit?

Can you see everything you want with one glance?

The fact is, if we compare what our eyes can see to what our eyes can't see, we could be considered 'almost blind'.

Don't be shocked! This is the truth.

Look, according to scientists' rough

calculations, we live in a universe that has a radius of 15 million light years.

Everyone knows this is a big number, but it's hard to understand just how big.

We will never know 70 percent of this 15 million light year radius universe. We can't see it! Scientists have called this 70 percent "dark energy."

From the 30 percent left, 25 percent of it is dark matter! We can never see this thing called dark matter either.

So what's left is five percent.

See, everything we see and hear is in this five percent.

But, don't hurry to say, "that's good!"

Because, the human eye can't even see all of that five percent. We can barely see a fragment of it.

Like I said before, when faced with the universe we could be considered almost 'blind'.

In simpler words, with the most optimistic account, all our eyes can ever see in this universe is less than the area under an ants foot on the earth's crust.

Now, since we can't even see the universe we live in properly, how is it possible to see the creator of this universe who doesn't look anything like His creation?

Allah can't be seen directly

Some people say, "I won't believe in something I don't see", "I don't believe in what I don't see, since I don't see Allah, I don't believe in Allah!"

This is an incredibly absurd thing to say, because there are so many things we don't see but we are sure they exist.

Let's quickly look at some of them:

GRAVITY

THE MIND

HAPPINESS

LOVE

THOUGHTS

You know what all these are, right?

But, you haven't seen any of them with your eyes. Therefore, we don't always have to see everything.

Just because we can't see something, doesn't mean it's not there.

Although we can't see Allah, we know He is our Creator and we believe in Him.

We don't have to see Allah to believe in Him!

We don't have to see Allah to believe in Him. Let me try to explain this to you with an example.

Come on, let's go to an art gallery. Look at the beautiful paintings by artists.

There's a huge canvas on that wall! The canvas is covered with daisies, with gold hearts adorning a little hillside.

Above the hill is a blue sky covered with clouds as white as the daisies.

What's more, there are brown birds flying in the sky. So many birds...

And, in the distance, a lush green forest...

Now, I'm going to ask you some questions. You're going to find some of the questions absurd. But still, you should answer them!

"Isn't this a beautiful painting?"

"Oh it is!"

"Who made this painting?"

"An artist of course."

"Did you see the artist?"

"No!"

"Then how do you know an artist made it?"

"Because there's no other way! I know because only an artist could have made such a painting."

"But you didn't see the artist!"

"But I've seen the painting. I have seen the daisies, the sky, the brown birds and the clouds! It's impossible for these things to occur on their own."

"Alright, if the paints and paint brushes lay there on the table for a while, could they decide to make a painting one day? And couldn't they do it once they made their decision?"

"You said your questions were going to be a little absurd, but I wasn't expecting this much. Never mind a painting, a single brush stroke wouldn't come about in this way."

"Are you sure?"

"I'm pretty confident. There needs to be an artist for such a painting to be made."

"But the artist isn't around. Could they be on the painting somewhere?"

"Is that possible? What would the artist be doing in the painting? The artist would be outside the painting."

"What about the paint and brushes? Could the artist be one of them?"

"You're being silly. Even if the brushes and paints lay there for millions of years, they couldn't think of making a painting like this."

"Why?"

"Because they don't have the brains! Because they don't have the ability! Because they aren't alive!"

"Those are great answers."

Come on, let's get out of the gallery now.

Now we are at the bottom of a little hill. Look at this place! We're surrounded by daisies. The sky is so blue. And the blue sky is covered with white clouds. Clouds as white as daisies!

And look at those birds tweeting, look how happy they are as they fly.

"Doesn't this place look a lot like the painting we just saw?"

"Yes, but this is more beautiful. Everything here is so vibrant."

"Do you think this scene is more beautiful than its painting?"

"Of course this scene is better."

"Well, if it's not possible for that painting to occur on its own, is it possible for this scene to come into existence on its own?"

"Of course not, it was created by..."

"Wait! Don't answer yet."

Now, look around you carefully! Don't say anything for a while and listen to me.

Come, let's look closer; let's observe the golden-centred daisies more closely. Let's count their leaves. Let's look at their colours. Look how well the yellow and the white go together.

And what about the green grass? What a beautiful spring carpet.

Look, there are bees dancing on some of the

flowers.

Hardworking ants are running from branch to branch.

Take a deep breath! Isn't that a nice scent?

And what about that bright poppy?

Where else can you find such a colour?

How about that butterfly's wings? Look! Look closely! But don't touch. It's so delicate...

Let's lie on our backs, on the flowery carpet and watch the sky.

The sky, the blue sky!

The clouds, as white as daisies!

The swallows flying over us and the storks with their broad wings.

There's a forest in the distance.

Do you see every tone of green on the trees?

The trees are so beautiful.

All right, now tell me! If you think it's impossible for this to be made without an artist, can you say it came into existence on its own?

"No! No! Never! These are all of Allah's creations."

"But you can't see Allah!"

"What difference does it make? I can see the flowers, the sky, the bees, and the butterflies He created! I can see the blue sky.

"I take in the beautiful fragrance of the flowers.

"I touch the daisy's cool leaves.

"I count the clouds.

"I watch the birds passing by, flapping their wings.

"Even if I don't see Allah, I believe in Him as if I see Him. All of these beautiful things and other beautiful things on this earth are His masterpiece."

One last question

Now, a question like this may come to your mind, "Okay, we can't see Allah. But, if Allah wanted, couldn't He make Himself visible to us?"

I told you at the beginning that you were right in wanting to see and know Allah.

Yes, all of Allah's servants want to see him.

They wonder, "Who is our Lord? What is He like?"

And Allah fulfils our curiosity. He shows Himself to us in the way He wants. But not in this world. In heaven.

The Prophet, peace be upon him, says:

"When those deserving of Paradise would enter Paradise, He (the narrator) would ask:

'Allah made a promise to you; now He wants to fulfil it.'

They say, 'Hast Thou not brightened our faces? Hast Thou not made us enter Paradise and saved us from Fire?'

Then, He (God) would lift the veil, and of things given to them nothing would be dearer to them than the sight of their Lord, the Mighty and the Glorious!"

Remember what I said to you at the start of this book:

If there is a question, there is definitely an answer!

How great is Allah?

WHO KNOWS HOW many times you have heard, "Allah is great!" And now you ask, "Yes, but how great?"

I will try to answer this question in depth but without boring you. But still, you must be patient, and read this chapter to the end.

First, here's a question for you:

You are taller than your sibling. But how much taller?

Let's say you are 150 cm and your sibling is 100 cm.

150-100=50

That means you are 50 cm taller than your sibling.

It was easy to find how tall you were - right?

Yes, it was easy! Because we could compare your height with your siblings. In this way, we could calculate the height difference and immediately answer the question.

Now, I expect you to have understood that: to understand "how big" something is, we need to compare one thing with another thing.

For example, to see how much taller you are than your sibling, we had to compare both of your heights.

Now, let's go back to our topic, "How great is Allah?"

Now, you tell me, what can we compare Allah with? What can we compare Him with and say, "He's that big or this big"? Nothing of course!

So, when a question like, "How great is Allah?" comes to mind, or if someone asks us such a question, first we have to know this: this question is wrong.

You can't find a correct answer to a wrongly asked question. Just like we can't open our house door with the wrong key.

So, the first thing that needs to be done is to ask the right question.

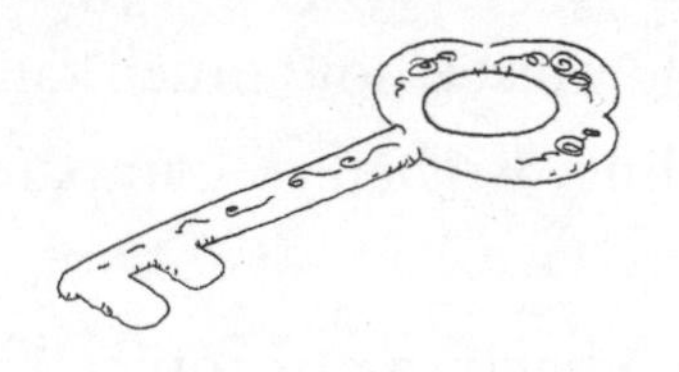

How can we describe Allah?

The greatness of oceans, continents, the world, the Sun, the solar system and galaxies is not the same as Allah's greatness.

First, all of these things are only great compared to some things. And they are small compared to other things.

However, Allah is just great.

For example, your height is greater than your brother or sister's height.

But your height is smaller than your dad's.

This means, that your height is not truly great.

See, the greatness of everything we see and every being ever created in this endless universe, is like the greatness of your height.

Mountains are great but oceans are greater.

Oceans are great but the world is greater.

The world is great, but the Sun is greater than the world.

And the Sun might be great, but there are much much much greater stars in space.

And, of course, Allah, who creates all of these, is great.

But His greatness is not like the greatness of the mountains, oceans, the world, the Sun or even the endless universe. All these things are small or big according to each other.

As for Allah, He is greater than everything and everyone. Nothing is greater than Him.

Allah's greatness is unimaginable

Our world, with its continents, oceans, mountains, orbits around the Sun.

And the Sun is one million three thousand times bigger than the Earth.

In the Milky Way galaxy, where the Sun is, there are 200 billion other stars like the Sun, most of which are even bigger.

And in the depths of space, further than humans can see, there are 250 billion other galaxies like the Milky Way.

Since the universe in which we live in is so great, Our Lord, Allah, who created the universe and the stars, is so great that it's impossible for us to understand.

Understanding Allah's greatness

What do you think of when I say, "Saladin was a great man?" You don't think something like, "He was 30 metres tall, and his arms were 5 metres. And don't even ask about his feet, they were enormous", right?

Wait, wait! Don't rush. I'm not mocking you. Also, my sense of humour is not that bad. My strange words have a serious link with our topic.

When we say, "Saladin was a great man", we mean he was a great ruler, one of the most famous of Muslim heroes and other achievements which meant his name was written in history.

Therefore, the word GREAT in this sentence doesn't mean what we first think of from the word GREAT.

Saladin is great and so are the mountains.

But the greatness of Saladin and the mountains are quite different.

What you should understand from this simple example is that there is a difference from one "great" to another.

When you hear "Allah is great", don't think of his actual being but think of his creation. Because He, who was there when nothing was, is not like any other thing. Our minds can never know, understand or think of Allah's being.

When you think of Allah's creation, you may understand Allah's greatness like you should.

Of course, Allah, who operates billions of cells in your body, is great.

Allah, who brings out the most delicious fruits out of rocks and mud, is great.

Allah, who makes billions of flowers smile all at once, is great.

Allah, who transports seas of water in clouds and pours it in droplets wherever he wants, is great.

Allah, who makes the Earth orbit around the Sun at 108.000 km/h (30 kilometres per second!) without letting even a single butterfly get dizzy, is great.

Everything you see when you open your eyes shows you Allah is great.

Birds flying, people walking, tigers running, trees growing, fishes swimming, flowers blossoming, winds blowing, stars shining, babies smiling, mother's love, children talking – everything shows us Allah's greatness! Because all of these are an example of a big miracle and are great things that no one but Allah can make happen.

Yes, our Lord Allah, is great!

His capability is enough for everything! His capability is great.

His workmanship creates all beauty. His workmanship is great.

His compassion allows all living things to be fed. His compassion is great.

He sees everyone and protects everyone. His sight is great.

He hears every voice, hears every prayer. His hearing is great.

He is our Lord, Allah. And Allah is great!

Allahu Akbar! God is Great!

Every prayer time, the *adhan* starts with these words from the minarets:

Allahu Akbar!

Allahu Akbar!

Allahu Akbar!

Allahu Akbar!

Every Muslim starts prayer with these words:

Allahu Akbar!

They say "Allahu Akbar" and go into *ruku*.

They say "Allahu Akbar" and rise.

Again they say "Allahu Akbar", and go into sajda to Allah.

Then by saying "Allahu Akbar", they start the next rak'ah.

Hajji's greet the Ka'bah by saying "Allahu Akbar". During the Eid prayer, we all say "Allahu Akbar" repeatedly...

The most common thing Muslims say is "Allahu Akbar".

When we are scared, "Allahu Akbar"!

When we are happy, “Allahu Akbar”!

When we are amazed, we say “Allahu Akbar”!

“Allahu Akbar” can be translated in its closest meaning as, ‘Allah is greatest’ in English. However, this doesn’t mean others are not great but Allah is the greatest.

Everything I’ve been trying to explain to you, from the start of this chapter, is that Allah’s greatness is not like the greatness of other great things we know.

Allah is great. There are no others who are truly great, other than Allah.

Where is Allah?

ALLAH IS BOTH nowhere and everywhere. In this chapter, I will explain to you what I mean by these words that may confuse you at first. Therefore, you will find out the answer to the question, "where is Allah?"

For a fish, it's not possible to get out of the water. Let's say there was a fish whose mind worked as well as yours. It can think as much as it wants, it can't imagine itself out of the water, because, it's been in the water since the moment it came into existence. It doesn't know a different world. And because it doesn't know, its mind, imagination and thoughts are surrounded by water. For the fish, there is nothing outside of the water.

The water for the fish is what the ground is for you. For as long as you've known yourself, you have always been somewhere, in a location. There has never been a time when you weren't anywhere.

You were at home, in the street, at school, at a fairground...

You have been in a village, in a forest, in an orchard, in gardens, in different countries and cities.

When someone asked you, "where are you?" you have always had an answer. Because you definitely had to be somewhere. And this is why your mind asks you the question:

"So where is Allah? Doesn't He need to be somewhere too?"

This question is millions of times stranger than a fish asking you, "Which sea do you live in?"

The question "where" is for those like you and me who have been created out of atoms, cells, flesh and bones.

"Where is my pen?"

"Where is your house?"

"Where is Ahmad?"

"Where is Mount Arafat?"

"Where is the Pacific Ocean?"

"Where is the Moon?"

"Where is the North star?"

Because, objects, things made out of matter, have to be somewhere.

And, as Allah is nothing like His creation, he is neither an object nor a substance. For this reason, asking the question, "where is Allah?"

would not be appropriate. Because it doesn't have an answer.

Allah doesn't have an obligation to be somewhere, like us. Allah doesn't have an obligation for anything.

For you to understand this even a tiny bit, I will give you an example:

Some of Allah's creations are such that they are neither an object nor able to be held or seen. For example, think of your life. If I asked you, "Where are your lungs?" you would show me your chest.

Lungs have a place.

Your brain, kidneys, stomach, all have a place. But what about your life? In which part of your body is your life?

You can't see it!

This is because life is not an object, so it doesn't have a place in your body. It doesn't have to be somewhere. In one sense it's all over your body, in another, it's nowhere.

What you can understand from this example is, the further something is from being an object, the harder it will be to answer the question of "where is it?".

So, if we can't ask the question "where" for something like life, which Allah created, we can't ask this question about Allah.

Nowhere and everywhere

Allah created Space, the stars, the Sun, the World, seas, forests, continents, in fact, everything. These were not there before. But Allah was. This means Allah was there when nothing else was. This means Allah was nowhere. Because "anywhere" didn't exist.

Yes, at the start of this chapter, I said, "Allah is nowhere and everywhere". I hope that what you have read up to here is enough for you to understand that Allah is nowhere.

But now you're asking:

"How can the One who's nowhere be everywhere?"

Now I'm going to give you another simple example. You can think of these examples as a telescope that shows you distant things as close up.

Issues that our minds may struggle to see (understand) may be seen (understood) easily with the help of these telescopes (examples).

This is why examples are important.

Now think of the Sun.

Our bright lamp in the sky, which brightens our world every morning when it rises.

Everywhere is bright once the Sun rises.

The Sun shows itself everywhere.

It's as if you can see a sparkling sun everywhere you look.

On the cool morning dews on the roses...

On the flowing water of creeks.

On the windows of houses.

In the eyes of people, cats, birds.

The Sun brightens everything and everyone. It shows on everything and everyone.

But, where is the Sun in reality?

In the sky!

But if we say, "there's a piece of the sun on all these things with its light and heat," we wouldn't be lying. Indeed, the Sun is everywhere it shines.

But, at the same time, it's in none of those places.

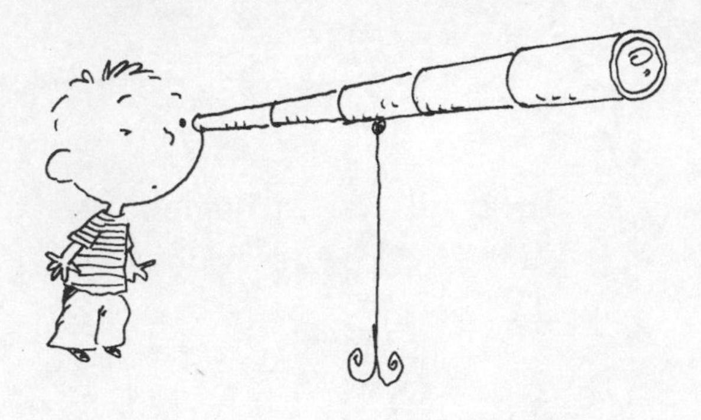

Just like the sun's heat and light is on every window, every eye, on every particle of frost, on every piece of sand, on every snowflake, on every water droplet, it is not actually in any of these places, Allah is everywhere with His might, with His compassion, His knowledge, His ability, but He is nowhere with His being.

For example, Allah drives all the trillions of stars that orbit in their path without crashing into each other.

Allah's infinite might is on those stars.

For example, every baby born on the earth awaits sweet milk from their mother.

Allah's vast compassion is with all those babies.

For example, every spring, the countless flowers that blossom in every orchard and garden shows Allah's ability.

Allah's unique art is on the flowers.

Who created Allah?

IT WAS ABOUT a week ago. A family that came to our house had a cute daughter, about four years old.

She was nibbling like a squirrel on a big red apple that she had taken from the fruit bowl.

I asked her, "Hasn't Allah created a nice apple?"

She stopped nibbling, "Allah created this apple too?" she said.

"Yes!" I said. "Like all fruits, Allah created the apple, just for you."

And right after that statement, the hail of questions started. To be honest, I had started to sense where this was going.

"What about oranges?"

"Allah created oranges too!"

"Cherries?"

"Allah creates cherries as well!"

"Hazelnuts?"

"Hazelnuts too..."

"Tangerines?

"Hmm, pears?

"And, and, and ... watermelons!"

When she couldn't think of any more fruits, she went from plants to animals.

"Birds?"

"Allah created all the birds!"

"Storks?"

"Storks are also birds, so, of course, Allah created them too!"

"Ducks?"

"Allah created ducks too."

Fortunately, she didn't go through all the birds she knew. But, she continued to ask questions.

"Clouds?"

"Allah created clouds too!"

This question and answer thing was giving her a lot of pleasure. Before each question she giggled and got happy as if she was driving me into a corner with each question. Now, no one could stop the little girl, who really started to get joy out of this:

"Trees?

"Mountains?

"What about fish?

"People?

"Dogs?

"Jellyfish?

"Hair?

"Ribbons?

"Mum and dad?

"Grandpa and grandma?

After countless questions, she asked the question that I was waiting for:

"Ok then! Allah created everything. Then, then... then... who created Allah?"

Now, I had an answer. But, the problem was to explain it in a way this little girl could understand.

While I was trying to gather my thoughts, the little girl's dad jumped in, "Mmm, you can't ask such a question! And leave the man alone."

The little girl had no intention of leaving me alone. She shouldn't anyway. She turned to her dad and said, "But it came to me!"

That's it! The question came to her mind. What could she do? Since the question came to her mind, she must ask it.

I held her little hands and looked into her eyes and said:

"Well done! You are such a clever girl!" I also

told her, her eyes and hair were very beautiful. Like all little girls, she got embarrassed and a little spoilt. Of course, after all these compliments, she would listen to what I had to say.

"Look!" I said, "Allah created all of those things you said. But no one created Allah. Because He is Allah. Allah can't be created. He creates everything!"

My answer was short but I thought it would be enough.

The little girl's answer was also incredibly short. But for a four year old girl, it was more than enough:

"Hmmmm…"

The little girl didn't ask me any more questions. She went to my son's room where the toys were, while nibbling on the apple in her hand.

My answer had satisfied her.

At least for now...

I know the answer I gave to the little girl is not enough for you.

Well, I'm aware that I may have confused you by asking such a question. In that case, it's my duty to give you a satisfying answer.

As a matter of fact, the answer I gave to the little girl is more than enough for this question.

"Allah is the creator of everything. But He hasn't been created."

But, you may want some examples to really help you understand the answer.

Ok, there are two very good examples in a book I read. I think it will be enough to pass these on to you.

Where does the Earth get its light from?

From the Sun, of course!

Where does the Moon get its light from?

From the Sun as well!

Mars?

From the Sun!

Mercury, Venus, Jupiter?

From the Sun, from the Sun, from the Sun!

All right. Where does the Sun get its light from? Are you puzzled?

I'll repeat my question.

Where does the Sun get its light from?

From nowhere of course.

This is because the Sun is the source of light.

It warms and lights all the planets. But it doesn't get its heat or light from anywhere.

The meaninglessness of the question, "where

does the sun get it's light from?" is nothing compared to the meaninglessness of the question, "who created Allah?"

Here's another example from that book.

Think of a train with 10–15 wagons. Each wagon pulls the wagon behind it. And in the end, when we come to the engine, we can't say, "who pulls the engine?" Because if there wasn't an engine that pulls but isn't being pulled, the train wouldn't go.

These simple but enlightening examples show us that the question, "who created Allah?" shouldn't be asked.

A frog fell off the roof...

When I was in high school, my literature teacher wrote a strange poem on the board. Actually, I can't remember whether it was a poem or a nursery rhyme. But I haven't forgotten it after so many years:

A frog fell off the roof,
It quivered its tail!
The policeman who saw this said:
Write the following on my gravestone:
A frog fell off the roof,
It quivered its tail!
The policeman who saw this said:
Write the following on my gravestone:
A frog fell off the roof,

It quivered its tail!
The policeman who saw this said:
Write the following on my gravestone:
A frog fell off the roof,
It quivered its tail!
The policeman who saw this said:
Write the following on my gravestone:
A frog fell off the ro...

Okay, okay, I'll stop now. Now, do you understand why I couldn't forget the frog and the policeman for so many years?

Well, what does this nonsense have to do with our question, "Who created Allah?"

Let's say we answered this question. Then the person who asked the question will say, "Well then who created Him?"

Let's say we answered this question too. The one who asked the question will ask another: "What about Him?"

"And Him?"

"And what about the one that came before that?"

And this would go on eternally, without

reaching an exact and correct answer.

A frog fell off the roof,
It quivered its tail!
The police who saw this...

Now, do you see the link between the nursery rhyme and our topic? Both of them are nonsense and lack an ending.

Now, let's remember the answer to the little girl's question:

"Allah created all of those things you said. But no one created Allah. Because He is Allah."

Yes, Allah is the creator. So He has not been created. And He can't be created.

Since Allah is the Creator, He is our Lord. This is why we can't ask, "Who created Him?"

Because, the Creator can't be created.

Look how our Lord introduces Himself in the Qur'an:

In the name of God, the Lord of Mercy, the Giver of Mercy

Say, "He is God the One, God the eternal. He does not give birth, He was not born. No one is comparable to Him."

Surah Al-Ikhlas 112:1-4

Do you know what happened before Allah sent this surah to Prophet Muhammed, peace be upon him?

Some people came to the Prophet and asked, "If Allah created everything, who created Allah?"

They were not little kids, they were adults. The Prophet got very angry at grown adults asking such questions on purpose.

And as a reply to this, Allah sent this surah with Angel Gabriel.

What kind of a being is Allah?

IT'S A GOOD thing that you wonder about Allah and don't hesitate to ask the questions that come to your mind. I'm constantly saying that it's completely normal for someone to wonder about Allah, the One who created everything. It's even abnormal not to.

We should wonder about Allah and try to learn. Questions like, what kind of a being is He, why did He create us, what does He want from us, how can we get to know Him better and how can we thank Him for all the good things He gave to us, should be asked by everyone and they should search for the answers.

But you must never forget something: our mind has a limit. The capability of our understanding can only help us to some extent. It cannot go beyond that.

When I was your age, I read some books that confused me. And I couldn't find proper answers to the questions I had about Allah.

What is He like?

What does He look like?

Where is He?

At the time, I didn't have a book that would answer such questions. (You see, I was not as lucky as you are!) I didn't know anyone who could answer these questions either.

I started to think, *since my mind doesn't understand Allah, why should I believe in Him!?* So, isn't it completely normal for someone to not believe something they don't understand?

One day, I was alone at home. I was sitting on the window ledge watching dozens of poplar trees swaying in the wind.

I suddenly started asking myself some questions:

Where am I?
In my room.
Where is my room?
In my house.
Where is my house?
In our street.
What about the street?
In our neighbourhood of course.
Neighbourhood?
In Istanbul.
Istanbul?
In Turkey.
Turkey?
Somewhere on the Earth! Where else?
The Earth?
In the Solar System!
Solar System?
In the Milky Way galaxy.
What about the Milky Way? Where is that?
In Space.
What about Space?
Space?
Yes, the thing called Space, or the place, or

whatever it is, where is it?

I don't know. Maybe it's in another space.

Then what about that other space?

Well, I'm confused. I don't know. No one knows this.

Correct! That's the answer! No human could answer this question.

Therefore, I can't deny Allah just because I don't understand Him.

My mind will never understand some things.

Some things won't ever be understood by anyone. Some things won't be understood even if all humans' minds came together.

Since we don't understand the universe we live in, of course it's impossible for us to understand the One who created the universe: Allah, who made it exist.

I was trying to fit a whole ocean into a tiny little egg. Was this realistic?

Today, as I recalled this memory, I said, "One feels so confident in one's teenage years." Because, to uncover the limits of my mind, I didn't need to stroll around the limits of space. It would have been enough to have stayed inside my mind.

We still don't know how the human brain, with billions of nerve cells contacting each other, works. The human mind hasn't even solved the mysteries of the brain and mind. Our mind doesn't understand our mind!

If we're going to deny Allah because we don't understand Him, we need to deny our minds first. Because we can't understand that either!

As I grew up, I realised there were so many things my mind wouldn't be able to figure out, like my soul and my life.

No one even understood what kind of a thing our soul and life was.

So, with such a mind, it's impossible for us to understand Allah.

Besides, Allah doesn't expect us to understand. But we could get to know Him and understand His existence and oneness and what kind of God He is.

This is why Allah created us. We need to get to know Him, love Him and worship Him.

The universe is a book

There are three big guides that introduce us to our Lord. First is our Prophet, second is the holy Qur'an and the third is this universe.

Imagine it's a lovely day, come let's try to read some of the pages of this universe-book. Let's see and learn what this huge book will tell us about Allah.

The largest and most spectacular page of this book is the sky.

Don't you see how the dark curtain of the night is decorated with billions of stars?

There's neither a rope nor a pole holding these stars up! Yet, not even a little tent can stay upright without a rope or a pole.

Allah is the One who holds them in emptiness and rotates them in their path without crashing into one another.

So, on this star covered page, it is written that our Lord has infinite power.

Now, let's look at the surface.

It's as if, on this day, a carpet decorated with countless flowers has been rolled out onto orchards and gardens. This spring page with flowers, each one more beautiful than

the other, informs us of our Lord Allah's craftsmanship.

If we read this flower-covered page carefully, we will feel like saying, "Allah, if the flowers you created are so beautiful, who knows how beautiful you are?"

Now let's look at the various sweet fruits on the trees' branches.

Apples, cherries, colourful plums, one sweeter than the other... Haven't all of these fruits been presented to us from the branches of this tree that drinks muddy water from its roots?

As well as showing us how much our Lord loves us, these also show us how much compassion He has to feed the beings He created.

If He wanted, Allah could just feed us with mud.

Now let us look at the animals. Do you see how many animals there are on this page?

Cows that eat grass to give us delicious milk, buzzing honeybees, birds that fly so easily by flapping their wings.

Don't all these animals say what a great Creator Allah is?

Look, some of them have offspring. And look how each one looks after their offspring carefully.

Even the fiercest looking ones do not damage one hair on their offspring.

This means, their hearts have compassion. This means, He who created them in such a way is very compassionate.

Now let's look at one of the best pages. Let's find a mirror and stare at our face.

There are billions of faces in the world. And none of them are the same.

Allah created billions of different faces with a nose, two eyes, two ears and one pair of lips in a small amount of space.

The face-page tells us so many things about our Lord's unique workmanship. For example, Allah, who gives us an organ such as an eye, which lets us see, is definitely a God who can see. Allah, who blessed us with ears that can hear all sorts of sounds, can definitely hear all sounds.

This universe with its countless pages and infinite lines says so many things about Allah.

The universe is a huge book. We must read it and try to get to know Allah who shows Himself in the lines of this book.

Even though we may not understand Allah, we can understand what kind of a Creator He is and love Him more as we understand Him.

Why is there one God?

ALLAH IS ONE because there can't be another Allah. The most important aspect of our religion, Islam, is the ONENESS of Allah.

Everything in our religion starts with believing in the oneness of Allah.

There can't be two prime ministers in a country. For that matter, there can't even be two chiefs in a village. If there were, there would be chaos. When one says "come", the other would say "go", and when one says "go", the other would say "come".

You must have understood from this simple example that, if two rulers get involved in something, there will be chaos.

Everything in this universe works in a

certain order. The stars do not crash into each other, neither do the atoms. Everything flowing smoothly in such perfect order shows us Allah's oneness.

So, it's the same Allah rotating the stars so they don't crash, and the owner of all the atoms is the same Creator. The pen on that table doesn't randomly blow up like an atom bomb. Yes, I'm not exaggerating! What do you think would happen if the electrons in the atoms forming the pen crashed into each other?

Why do cars crash? Because there are different people driving each one! Each driver drives each car how they want. If one tried to go the same way that another was coming, there would be trouble! Why don't stars crash then? Because the same Allah makes all the stars move. As there is only one Allah who decides where each star goes, there isn't chaos in the sky. And, more stars than sand particles on this earth, orbit above our heads.

As there aren't two prime ministers in a country, two governors in a city, two chiefs in a town, the owner of this universe is also one. His oneness can be seen in everything.

Now I'm going to give you another example. But you have to listen carefully.

Allah created everything

Think of the furniture in your house. The sofas are from a certain company, the television is from another, the dining table and chairs are from another. The carpets have also been bought from a completely different place.

But this universe is not like that. Everything in this universe has the same tag: MADE BY ALLAH

Everything here from the fruits, to the trees, suns, birds and babies... anything you can think of, are linked so closely with each other, they can't be separated from one another. Whoever created one of them, created all. Someone else can't come and say, "I created this one."

So that you can understand this, I will give you the "glass of milk" example. It's a question and answer game. I'll ask and you answer:

"How did the glass of milk on the table get there?"

"My mum brought it from the fridge."

"Okay, how did it get in the fridge?"

"I bought it from the shop yesterday."

"Where did the shop find that milk?"

"Hmmm... Well there are factories for this stuff. It must have come from there."

"Okay, you're doing great. Well then, where did the factory find that milk?"

"There's such a thing as a dairy farm. From there."

"Where does the dairy farm get the milk from I wonder?"

"Where else, from cows!"

"And the cows?"

"The milk is produced in the udder of cows, who eat grass all day."

"Where's the grass from?"

MILK

"The grass is from the soil. It's all very green once it's spring."

"In that case, you need to explain how and where spring comes from!"

"When the earth orbits the sun, seasons appear. Spring is a season. That's how."

"Okay. Now let's join the start of our game with the end. For a glass of milk to appear at your table, the earth needs to orbit the Sun!"

"That's so true!"

"In that case, to create a glass of milk, don't we need to create the Sun as well?"

"Yes, one who can't create the Sun also can't create a glass of milk."

"Then this shows us that the true owner of a glass of milk is also the owner of the Sun."

Everything is connected

Everything in this universe is interconnected. One thing can't happen without the other happening.

So this is how a glass of milk teaches us about Allah's oneness.

Now, think of a single fly. It's eyes need the sun to see. This means the sun's light and the fly's eye have been created to suit one another. Therefore, whoever created the fly also created the sun. Because they are both suited to one another, this job can only be done by the One who knows about both of them.

The creator of the fly cannot be different from the creator of the sun. Both the fly and the sun are Allah's creation.

Just like in this example:

Whoever created the birds also created the air. Because those birds can only fly in this air. This means, the One who created the birds, the birds' wings and each feather on those wings, also created the atmosphere.

Now you can find examples from fruits, trees and your own body. Whatever you think of will show you Allah's oneness. Because everything in this universe is connected to each other and shows the One. Just like a glass of milk and like a fly's eye.

How can Allah do so many things at once?

MANY OF THE questions about Allah come to us because we think of Allah within our own limits.

We ask: "I can't do it, so how does Allah do it?", "I can't do two things at once, how does Allah do countless things at once?"

Correct! You can't look in two different directions at once.

You can't say two separate words at once, or hear two words that are being said to you at once. Even if you hear it, you don't understand.

Your body and your mind have limits.

But when spring comes, billions of flowers bloom overnight.

While the flowers bloom, countless birds hatch out of countless eggs.

While the birds slowly grow in eggs, billions of seeds split in the soil.

While the seeds slowly sprout, rain droplets are being created in the depths of clouds.

While the rain pitter-patters onto the surface, thousands of mothers give birth to thousands of babies.

While the babies' first screams echo in the ears of their mothers, there are countless explosions on the sun.

Thousands of meteors fall on the moon and children happily point out to each other the colourful rainbow that appears in the blue sky.

While the shimmering rainbow smiles, billions of little fish move their fins for the first time, metres under the sea.

As the fish speed away from colourful coral rocks, a father happily watches his son's first steps.

A lion is roaring; an antelope's heart is beating steadily; a pearl is appearing in an oyster.

A canary is singing for the first time, an elephant is taking its last breath in the depths of the jungle.

An old and playful crow, is trying to break the shell of the walnut he stole.

As it turns to morning in one place, the sun sets in another.

One child is having a dream, while another is saying, "Good morning, Mum!"

As billions of cells die in your body, billions are being created.

Blood is flowing through your veins, your heart is beating and your nerve cells are sending each other a message.

A shooting star flies past.

In the sky, angels are smiling!

All at the same time.

And you ask, "How does Allah do all these things and create all these things at the same time?"

If you look around you carefully, you will see that some of Allah's creation is made to do more than one thing at once.

In that case, our Lord, with his infinite power and capacity, creating infinite things and doing infinite things at once, won't be such an incomprehensible state.

For example, think of Allah's sun.

When the sun rises, it brightens everyone and everything at once.

Every word coming out of a man's mouth in front of tens of thousands of people goes to everyone's ear at once.

Gravity pulls down everything on the earth at once.

All of these things happen due to laws created by Allah. In that case, Allah doing infinite things and creating infinite things at once, like the sun brightening everyone at once; like a word being heard by thousands of people at once; like gravity pulling everything down at once, is easy.

Allah says, "BE," and it is.

When We will something to happen, all that We say is, "Be," and it is.

Surah Al-Nahl 16:40

Allah creates spring as easily as He creates a flower.

Allah rotates planets as easily as He rotates atoms.

Allah makes all people live as easily as he makes one person live.

Small jobs are easy, big jobs are hard. But this is only for us.

For Allah, both small and big are one.

For Allah, a little bit and a lot are the same.

For Allah, a thousand doesn't make a difference.

There isn't a difference between heavy and light for Allah.

Because Allah says, "BE!" And whatever He wants happens!

Now I'm going to give you an example so that you can understand this better

You know how to write. I mean, you can bring letters together and write words and sentences.

Now tell me, is it easier to take the pen and write ONE or MILLION?

Did you say, "What difference does it make?"

But one is ONE; the other is MILLION. Wouldn't it matter?

Of course it wouldn't matter! For someone who knows how to write, there's only a few letters difference between writing ONE and writing MILLION.

Writing ONE is only a little bit easier than writing MILLION.

Ok then, is there a difference between writing SMALL and BIG?

Is SMALL easier to write because it's small, and BIG harder to write because it's big?

For someone who knows how to write, there is barely any difference between writing SMALL and BIG. They are both easy.

Now look at the window of this small example; you will see a great truth.

For Allah, who creates from non-existence, there's no difference between creating something small and something big.

There's no difference between creating one thing and creating millions of things.

An atom, or a planet; a flower, or millions of flowers, it's all the same for Allah.

Once Allah says, "BE," whatever he wants happens. If Allah wants, He creates one, if He wants, He creates a million.

If Allah wants, He could create small or big.

He creates a flower.

He creates a tree.

He creates spring.

He creates heaven.

For Allah, they're all the same.

He creates an atom.

He creates a fly.

He creates a mountain.

He creates the earth.

As He creates billions of flies, he also creates billions of stars.

It's all the same for Allah.

Once Allah says, "BE," whatever he wants happens.

Everything obeys Allah

Nothing would happen if you said, "Be." If I said, "Be," again, nothing would happen. If we all said, "Be," together, again, nothing would happen.

If we got a handful of soil and said, "Be a flower," it wouldn't be a flower.

If we got an egg in our hand and said, "Be a bird!" it wouldn't grow wings and fly.

If you say to the clouds in the sky, "Be rain!" not even a single drop of rain would fall on us.

If we said to tree branches, "Be fruit," they wouldn't be.

No matter how many times we say, "Be,"

nothing would happen.

Because we are not the owners of those things. We didn't create them.

A tree branch wouldn't listen to us because we didn't put the branch on the tree trunk. We are also not the ones that brought the tree up from the depths of the soil from a little seed. We are also not the ones that created the tree with its trunk, bark and leaves. The tree wouldn't listen to us, nor would its branches.

Eggs wouldn't turn to birds and fly because we said, "Be."

But if Allah says "BE," everything will happen.

You probably can't imagine this happening. But that's because you've never been in the military. Every army has a general. When the general says, "Stop!" everyone stops.

When the general says, "Run!" everyone runs.

When the general says, "Lie down!" everyone lies down.

When the general says, "Come!" everyone

comes.

Because he is a general, everyone in the army listens to his command and performs it.

If I said, "Run!" to the same army, no one would move a muscle. If I shout, "Come!" everyone would laugh.

Because I'm not a general, my words wouldn't apply to the army. In the army, the general's words apply.

Come now, look through the window of this simple example at the universe. You will see that Allah's commands apply to this universe, because he is the Sultan of this palace. Everything listens to His command and obeys.

Whatever is in the sky and on the ground is His and they only move with His command.

Things that wouldn't happen with us saying, "be," happen with His command.

Allah says, "BE," and fruits appear on branches.

Allah says, "BE," and flowers appear in gardens.

Allah says, “BE,” and honey appears in honeycombs.

Allah says, “BE,” and the rain and snow appears in clouds.

Allah says, “BE,” and babies appear in mother’s tummies.

Allah says, “BE,” and a seed’s case splits.

Allah says, “BE,” and a little shoot sprouts from the open case of the seed.

Allah says, “BE,” and that little shoot pushes out into daylight, pushing aside the stones and soil on top of it.

Allah says, “BE,” and that little shoot that came into the daylight, starts to grow.

It grows and grows and grows.

And Allah says, “BE,” and that shoot turns into a tree.

The tree grows branches and then fruits grow on the branches.

The fruits get taste, smell, colour, shape.

Whatever happens is because Allah says, “BE!”

He is the owner of everything, and He is our Lord.

...Everything in the heavens and earth belongs to Him, everything devoutly obeys His will. He is the Originator of the heavens and the earth, and when He decrees something, He says only, "Be," and it is.

Surah Al-Baqarah 2:116-17

Everyone in the heavens and earth belongs to Him, and all are obedient to Him.

Surah Al-Rum 30:26

It is to God that everything in the heavens and the earth truly belongs...

Surah Yunus 10:55

Why does Allah create trees to create fruit?

WHAT'S THE NEED? Right? What's the need of trees, once Allah has wanted to create apples?

The apples could have easily fallen from the sky like rain!

Or they could have suddenly appeared like frost particles on grass.

Why does Allah create a tree to create an apple?

This time, you really asked a solid question. But don't worry, I have a truly solid answer.

As you know, Allah isn't dependent on a tree to create an apple, just like He isn't dependent on a cow to create milk or on a bee to create honey. If Allah wanted, He could create an apple without a tree, milk without a cow and

honey without bees.

If Allah wanted, apples could suddenly appear in between blades of grass.

In the morning, we would find bottles of milk in front of our door, and we would never know where it came from.

And if Allah wanted, He could make bucket loads of honey rain down from the sky...

But Allah doesn't do this.

Whatever He creates, he offers it to us through the hands of reason.

They're sent through the hands of trees for apples, cows for milk and bees for honey.

Okay, but why?

Why does Allah create in this way but not the other way?

Everything happens for a reason!

Of course, there's a reason behind Allah creating everything on earth with a number of causes.

We look at Allah's creation to get to know Him. In this way, we can understand what kind of a Lord He is.

If Allah had not created everything through reasons, had created them without a reason, we wouldn't be able to understand our Lord's greatness so well.

For example, If Allah had not made trees bear fruit, we wouldn't be able to see how those sweet apples grow from the tree branches.

We humans can only make furniture like tables and chairs from wood. Yet Allah makes fruits from wood.

I don't know if you have ever tried this. You might want to try it one day. Bite a branch on an apple tree and taste it! But don't try to eat it! Let alone not being able to taste apples, you will get a bitter taste in your mouth.

That bitter and tasteless wood is the thing

that produces the delicious apples you enjoy. If Allah had not created those fruits from those bitter branches, we wouldn't be able to see such a miracle. And we wouldn't be able to understand the greatness of our Lord's art.

We wouldn't have a chance to say, "Allah, you create such delicious fruit for us from the bitter and tasteless wood."

And think about milk. The sweet, white milk that flows between the blood and waste that would be thrown out once digested and that hay and water inside a cow's stomach.

If Allah hadn't offered the milk to us by making cows, we wouldn't be able to witness this extraordinary happening. Yet, isn't it really interesting for milk to be created through such weird causes. What a huge miracle it is!

Don't worry, I'm not going to say to you,

"Get some hay and grass, and mix them with some water and taste it, is it like milk?"

What about honey? Allah made a bee, a tiny bug with a poisonous needle stuck on it, the cause for the sweet honey.

If you had no knowledge about honey, could you imagine that an insect with a poisonous needle had made it? You definitely couldn't.

Just like you couldn't have guessed that cherries come from tasteless wood and perfectly white milk from cows' stomachs, you would also not be able to guess that honey is made by bees.

Come now, let's think of those birds. Allah could have created those amazing creatures, flapping their wings in the sky, just like 'that'. But then, none of us would see a tiny bird come out of a lifeless egg. We wouldn't be able to watch Allah turn those thousand and one eggs into swallows flying with their swanky tails, little sparrows, pigeons with copper eyes, beautiful seagulls, spectacular peacocks, blond canaries, beloved doves and those egg machines; the chickens.

Think about all the food we eat. Wheat, potatoes, beans, tiny little peas, grapes on vines, watermelons and melons on vegetable patches; just imagine it all. Our Lord has made the soil, water and air a reason for all these delicious foods.

These three substances; soil, air and water, that don't know us or the needs of our stomachs, have been created as a cause for all food.

Now let's look at that tasteless dark soil, water that flows to wherever you lead it, and the air. Then let's think about all those fruits and vegetables once more, or even thousands more times. Let's try to understand what kind of a Creator our Lord is.

If we had not seen these miracles come from such simple causes, we would never know Allah as well as we do now. We wouldn't know of his ability.

The reason for reasons

Now you are thinking of this question, "If there wasn't an explanation for things, and apple trees just appeared in an instance, wouldn't it be more interesting and a bigger miracle?"

It wouldn't!

The first time an apple instantly appears would of course surprise you. It would surprise everyone. Your eyes would open to the size of car tyres out of shock.

You would be surprised if you saw the same thing again. But not as much as the first time.

And on the third time, your surprise and astonishment would be much less.

And even less on the fourth time.

And on the hundredth time an apple instantly appears in front of your eyes, you would barely get surprised. You would say, "This is how it happens. It happens however it happens."

You would never wonder about how Allah made the apple, and as you wouldn't wonder, you also wouldn't know, learn or see.

Yet, every spring, watching dry branches come to life again, leaves turn green and delicious apples grow out of those dry branches, is an answer to the question, "how does Allah create an apple?"

Fortunately, there are reasons.

This is why there are causes. So we can see and watch our Lord's unique craft, step by step. Because all of these beautiful things, all of these miracles, fruit growing out of wood, milk dripping from cows' udders, tiny bees making honey, all inform us of our Lord's workmanship. It allows us to get to know Him better.

The sultan's ambassadors

As you know, when sultans or kings want to give someone a gift, they give the gift to their attendant and send it with them. Because it wouldn't suit a great emperor to give the gift himself.

Once upon a time, there was a man. He was poor and helpless. One day, someone knocked on his door. He opened the door and what should he see? A stranger with a variety of gifts in his hands, dressed in strange clothes!

The poor man was surprised. He said, "Who are you?"

The man said, "I am the ambassador of the Sultan. I brought you these gifts from his treasure, at his command. Take these and satisfy your needs!"

The poor man was so happy about this that he threw himself at the ambassador's feet. He hugged his feet and started kissing his hands and the skirts of his magnificent robe. He thanked him, blessed him and said many other complimentary things.

But the ambassador said, "What do you think you're doing? I am only the ambassador. You should be thanking the Sultan. You should give praise to the Sultan and say complimentary words to him. Think of his treasures and his generosity. Honour him, and obey him. I cannot give you these precious gifts, only he can."

The poor man who heard these words was a clever man, and he came to his senses. He immediately got to his feet and said, "Well done! This is how an ambassador should be. I didn't know what I was doing from happiness. You brought me to my senses. In fact, if I had looked at these presents properly, I would easily be able to tell they weren't your property. Of course an ambassador like you wouldn't have enough treasure to give out these gifts. These treasures are the Sultan's.

"Of course, I do respect you, and thank you. But the one I should actually be thanking is the Sultan. From now on, I will only praise his treasures and only talk about his generosity.

"I will repeat his name day and night and tell him my every need from now on.

"From now on, any gift that comes to my door or is given to me, I will know is from the Sultan. Because this whole country belongs to the generous Sultan."

Then, the ambassador left. He then took other precious gifts and knocked on the door of another man, and as he did with the first man, he gave the sultan's gifts to him.

This poor man, like the other one, kissed the ambassador's hands and feet and said many words of praise to him.

As for the ambassador, like with the previous man, he warned the second man. He told him these gifts didn't belong to him and he had brought them from the Sultan's treasure at the Sultan's orders.

However, this poor man wasn't as clever as

the one before. He didn't come to his senses, and he said, "Which Sultan are you talking about? I opened my door and saw you. If there were such a Sultan, he would have brought the gifts himself.

"I saw these precious things in your hands. Of course I won't thank anyone else. If I don't believe what my eyes see, what should I believe?

"There is no Sultan!"

Here the story ends. Now, let's look at what the moral of the story is.

Those trees reaching out their branches with a variety of fruit are just like that ambassador. Allah sends his endless treasures through their hands.

Some people, just like the first man, recognise the true Sender of these gifts and thank Allah, the Creator of the tree.

But some of them say, "I don't see a Sultan. I see these trees. These fruits are made by these trees. This is a natural thing." And like the man in the story, they only know ambassadors and only believe in ambassadors. They don't know Allah, the true Sender of blessings, and don't believe in Him.

Yet, our Lord, the Owner of this universe, the Creator offers numerous blessings to us through a variety of ways.

One of those ways is the trees, which are like the ambassador in our story. The ambassador said, "You should thank the Sultan, say words of praise to the Sultan. Think of his treasure, talk of his generosity; honour him and obey him! These precious presents can only be given by him, not me."

The tree, if it could, might say, "I'm a tree branch. What you know as wood. My roots are in dark soil. All I drink is muddy water!

"I don't have a mind or ability. Furthermore, I don't know you. I don't know what you enjoy, what your stomach and mouth is like.

"I don't know how useful these fruits growing on my branches are to you.

"What is taste, smell, colour, shape, skin, essence, seed, vitamin, I don't understand any of them.

"It's not possible for me to do those things. I am only a cause.

"You should protect me and treat me nicely. But don't come and thank me.

"These fruits, cherries, pomegranates, apples are not things I can create alone.

"Allah sends these gifts to you through my hands. Praise Him, thank Him, compliment Him, remember and celebrate His unique generosity.

"Don't ever forget your Lord, who feeds you with such beautiful fruits.

"Don't let your thoughts get stuck in me like kites tangled in my branches."

with it We produced for you gardens of date palms and vines, with many fruits there for you to eat

Al-Mu'minun 23:19

Let man consider the food he eats! We pour down abundant water and cause the soil to split open. We make grain grow, and vines, fresh vegetation, olive trees, date palms, luscious gardens, fruits, and fodder

Abasa 80:24-31

About the author

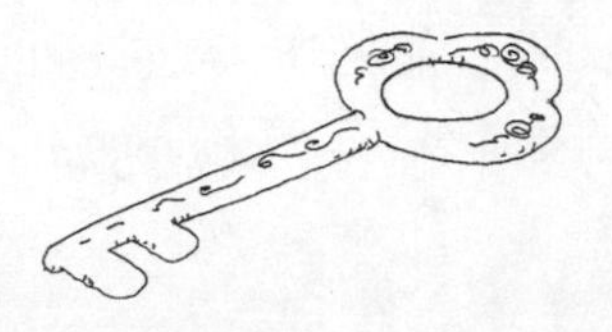

OZKAN OZE was born in Turkey in 1974. While at high school, he started working at Zafer Magazine's editorial office in Istanbul and discovered his love of literature and books. Sincc then he has gone on to become the editor of Zafer Publications Group and continually writes. He is married with two children.

Ozkan wrote the "I Wonder" Series because he believes that questions are prayers. Asking one is like saying, 'teach me to understand.' They act as keys that lead us through doors to new worlds, which are more interesting and beautiful than we thought possible.

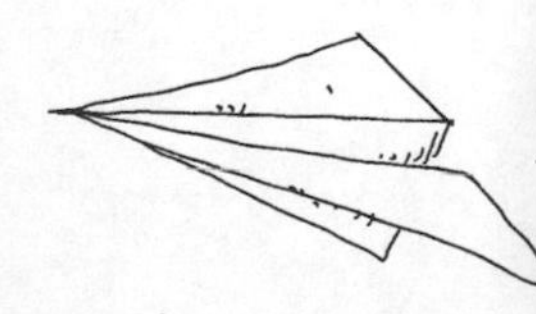

The “I Wonder” series

The “I Wonder” series give young readers answers to the BIG questions they have about Islam in brilliant little books. Written in a friendly and accessible style for today’s youth, these are essential companions for questioning young minds.

Books in the “I Wonder” series:

I Wonder About Allah (Book One)

I Wonder About Allah (Book Two)

I Wonder About the Prophet (Book Three)

I Wonder About the Qur’an (Book Four)

I Wonder About Heaven (Book Five)

I Wonder About Fate (Book Six)

I Wonder About Angels (Book Seven)